THE RAIN

ISAAC CURTIS-HARRIS

Copyright © 2023 by Isaac Curtis-Harris

First paperback edition published in 2023

Cover design and illustration by Nina C. Quintal

ISBN 979-8-3897-7969-3 (paperback)

1

It's raining again. It's a foregone conclusion. As predictable as night and day, that cyclic rolling of black to grey, then to black again. I actually can't remember the last time it wasn't like this. I stare out into the gaping blackness, barely able to identify the little needles of rain. It's dark out, so I strain my eyes and it hurts. Then I yawn, and this automatic bodily function brings about tears. They aren't tears of sadness I don't think, but they create a blurry lens through which I can view the world in dazzling swirls and shapes. It's rather beautiful, but I'm not usually one for tears, so it's a surprise when it occurs. It's not like watching the rain is the most exhilarating hobby in the world, but what else is there to do? This slight abnormality is a welcomed change.

The clouds are out and that means I'm staying in. What great news. I hear the baritone and clinical voice of the man on the television behind me spewing the usual buzzwords of "danger" and "risk" and I'm reassured that the decision to stay in my home is probably a smart one. I suppose that's just one of the side effects of this torrential rain we are privy to these days. I'm not complaining of course - it is the perfect excuse to avoid leaving the house. A part of me wishes that this house arrest was mandatory rather than self imposed. If I was forced to stay indoors, I'd be free of any responsibility over what happens. Should a tragedy occur, I'd simply be a victim of someone else's mistakes rather than a product of my own. No matter how severe the outcome of that mistake, I'd be fine with the consequences if it was due to someone else's failings. Does that make me strange? I guess everyone thinks of themselves as a little odd, it's a neat way to absolve oneself of the crime of having a shit mindset. Why should I attempt to try at all when 'people just don't get me'? Maybe we all have that feeling like nobody else really understands us. Therefore, it's probably not so weird that I absolutely refuse to leave my house, and who knows; maybe crippling fear of conversation doesn't hold up with others as an excuse, but avoiding an untimely end seems a much more valid reason to stay indoors. What with all the danger and the tragedy outside, it is probably the wisest and most measured decision to be in the position I am in. And, whilst I'm not one to pass up the opportunity to complain, I will admit that despite the implied danger, it's oddly serene when the rain is pouring down; the barely visible streets are completely empty, and aside from the rainfall; there isn't another sound. This emptiness – this complete lack of life outside could probably be seen as quite unsettling, but strangely, the absence of any other person out there is quite intimate. Just me and the pitter patter of the rain. Every cloud has a silver lining, right?

Perhaps it's not even for fear of conversation, but rather a fear that if I speak for long enough, people will realise that I actually have nothing to say. I sometimes imagine a terrifying scenario where I find myself speaking and surrounded by others while they just stare, waiting for me to slip up, hoping for that eventual mistake that they can pounce on. Not only are these little nightmares purely fictional, but I would also never give people the chance to take advantage of that opportunity. It's better to have people believe you're stupid rather than to open your mouth and remove all doubt, or something to that effect. More often than not, I'll loudly declare my stupidity – I'll scream it to the heavens! Professing my shortcomings is probably the first thing I would do if I were to meet someone new. It's not like I was ever taught this is the correct way to converse, in fact, the resultant and sparing conversations I've had throughout my life would suggest that this is precisely the opposite of what you should do if you want to be a good conversationalist or if you want to be at least somewhat likeable. If failure was a teacher of success, I would somehow be the only student to fail that class. I suppose it's no wonder why it's such a rarity for me to speak with others. In fact, I can barely remember the last time I met somebody new.

No - that is probably why I'm sat here on my own this miserable evening. That is probably why, despite the man on the news telling me I only need to stay indoors while the rain is coming down, I insist upon staying in on even the clearest of nights – not that I can recall there being a clear night. Perhaps if I was more interesting, or if I had something to say, I wouldn't be boring myself with this little rant - instead I'd be talking to a group of friends, or a wife - to anybody else. Maybe if I diagnose myself with one of those disorders that I've heard the newsman talk about, I won't have to take any responsibility for what is true: I am a coward. People would take pity; they might even think that I'm brave. But who am I kidding? That would require me to actually communicate that horrific and insulting idea to somebody else. And worse still, it would require me to maintain that charade to others. Screw it. I think the rain might even be better company than my own thoughts tonight. It's safer that way I reckon.

Then again, there's a certain tranquillity in listening to the rain. It reminds me of stories my father would tell me from his childhood where he'd run free and uncaring in the great outdoors. The rain wouldn't stop him, nothing could. I recall him telling me, without a hint of irony or sarcasm, how he would frolic and catch the rain on his tongue. That seems laughable now. He'd thunder through brambles and stinging nettles, knowing full well the damage they were capable of. Marching through puddles, chasing his friends in made up games, picking them up when they fell, fearing nothing; the world he lived in, despite its efforts to tear him down, would simultaneously nourish him and provide him with a sense of freedom and belonging. At least I think that's how it went. Those are just memories now – so is my father. And even when I think of these memories, even when I ponder those generically noble and admirable traits of his, I can't remember his face. I can barely even hear his voice. There is only the vague outline of a strong young man standing tall against the might of the elements. This outline itself is so faint, that I have no hope of attempting to trace that silhouette. There is simply no hope of following in the footsteps of this man who is now completely unrecognisable to me. I wonder if he'd recognise me.

The sound of the rain hitting my roof reminds me of those stories. It enables me to reflect on my current situation and to think about how much has changed. How trapped I am. It reminds me how little I can actually remember, it's like the rain has tapped the vision of those thoughts right out of me so that the only thing which remains is the rain. Those grainy black and white images in my head, replete with the cue marks and cigarette burns of an old newsreel, are now just a myriad of blurry shapes, completely alien to the eye. I try with all my might to think of those memories I never experienced, but over time the harder I try, the foggier they become.

I stand by the window and attempt to process every single rain drop as though they're each a delicate little memory, desperate to avoid being swallowed up by the next drop of water. Each one, clamouring to be recognised and validated. Each one, fighting for survival. I think about the futility of trying to recall memories that aren't my own. Are they even valid if they're someone else's? They're already unreliable when told in the first person – such is the imperfect nature of the human brain - but when I retell a memory to myself for the umpteenth time, when I in turn was told it by somebody else; how can I be sure that what I'm remembering is even remotely accurate? Each visit is edited with new details and forgotten incidents. How much is truth and how much is my attempt at filling in the gaps? Furthermore, how can I be sure that these stories even happened?

Because ultimately, that's all they are: stories. I could make up my own fantasies if that's the case. Is that so difficult? What, therefore, is the difference between fact and fiction? Am I a liar for indulging in these fantasies as though they're gospel, when I have no idea if they ever really occurred? I suppose the gentle joy of reminiscing about a time when things weren't as they are now makes it worthwhile, and if wrapping these stories in the warm blanket of nostalgia distracts from the truth – perhaps it doesn't matter if those stories are real or not. It's tiring work frankly, and I really don't have much energy these days. All that is certain, is that I am so sick of the rain.

While it's a delicate whisper tapping at the window, it's bearable. Some days, I would even go so far as to call it pleasant. It's repetitive and distracting, rhythmic and hypnotic, raw but soothing, and most of all - it's familiar. The rain is as omnipresent as the air I breathe, and while this stage of the evening can occasionally be somewhat enjoyable, I do not appreciate when the weather decides to deviate from the usual proceedings.

Up in the folds of darkness, the sky frowns and swells like it's trying to hold in a sneeze, until the little black wrinkles can't contain the pressure for any longer. Now it's the thunder's turn to take centre stage. In place of the repetitious beat of the raindrops, there comes the danger of irregularity. Its roar is deep and menacing like the guttural growls of some Lovecraftian monstrosity, the magnitude of which serves only as a reminder of my own insignificance. I look away from the window and back into my living room – and trust me, that is one of the more ironic uses of that word.

I have never seen a more barren room so bereft of life. I really can't remember it slipping into such a dishevelled state and it stuns me how quickly, albeit quietly, this place has deteriorated. I am actually a little bit ashamed, more than usual that is, and as I look from right to left at this ersatz little room of 'relaxation' I feel more shame climbing onto my already tired shoulders. With increasing disappointment, I am drawn to all the elements which make it so uncomfortable. On the back wall lies my sofa, bespeckled with the decaying dregs and memories of previous meals. Although it's fairly modest and only just about covers half the wall, its placement somehow makes the room feel crowded. Afront the sofa sits a dingy and weathered coffee table. It's small and square with sharp, but worn, corners. Furthermore, it's too low to be of sufficient use whilst sitting on the sofa, but cheap and tattered enough to earn its place in this gallery of glum. Adjacent to the table is my computer screen of a television set. I should probably choose my words more sensitively however, it's quite unreasonable for me to be so critical about the TV when it's been the closest thing to real company I have had.

During this solitude, it's acted as the only connection to the world outside and we have developed a bit of a love/hate relationship. While I may occasionally lament about my loneliness, I can't help but feel a bizarre combination of shame and relief whenever the reporter brings up more bad news. The mention of someone else's suffering is of course tragic, but it reminds me that my situation isn't so bad, and by comparison I am doing just fine. Sometimes I feel like the TV can hear what I'm thinking and addresses me personally. Obviously, I know that this is nonsense, however. Probably just a symptom of an overactive imagination. Besides, if my TV was any bigger, or had a higher screen resolution, it would not fit in with the rest of the mediocrity in here. It's all part of the scumbag décor, of course! As always, the news channel is on and right now the man is speaking about "safety" and "uncertainty". Not that I would actually listen to some newsman anyway, but the low buzz the TV emits when he speaks is another element of this isolation which has grown to be a comfort. His words no longer sound like coherent English but instead a low, monotonous drawl which is fulfilling its job of drowning out the onslaught on my house from above. I only occasionally pick out key words and interesting comments, or when the TV addresses me directly, other than that, it is purely background noise in a make-believe language. The colour and the sound the TV produces are more sympathetic brighteners to the room than the tall and flimsy lamp flanking my sofa, the harshness of which would seem more at home in an interrogation room.

But it's all I've got, so I shouldn't complain about it. The lightbulb dangling meekly from the ceiling above the coffee table, without its shade, is limp and lifeless and I don't dare go outside in this weather to replace it. It hasn't worked in ages. Not much in here has. Ironically the only breath of life in the room is the small patch of black mould perched in the corner of my ceiling like a nest of spider's eggs. Concerning – yes – but not something that I plan on giving any immediate attention. I guess it's no surprise that the only other living thing in my home is something I detest but have no intention of evicting.

During this inspection of the contents of my living room, the rain persists upon the roof and the window, until gradually, they cease to be individual taps of rain. Rather, drop by drop, they become one blunt object. And after being temporarily relegated to background noise, the rhythm of the rain picks up its intensity, and it is no longer peaceful or hypnotic. Instead, it has transformed into a far more sinister sound. The rain raps violently on my window in a ferocious display of power. This now terrible tool of misery, bombarding my home, demanding attention from me, recruiting more strength with each blow, threatens to knock down my defences and come inside…

BANG!

The thunder joins in again. And my attention is thrust back towards the window. There's no lightning though. That's weird.

BANG BANG!

Thunder has a strange quality about it. Even without it touching you, you can feel it through your entire body. Like any force of nature, its very existence is a demonstration of the weakness of man. Its presence is so strong. Its power is undeniable.

But even as the storm clouds bellow, sending shockwaves through my body, it feels so far away. Thunder always feels so distant. So impersonal.

It reminds me of observing a catastrophe from afar, you can't help but direct all your focus towards it, and yet you don't feel in immediate danger. Instead, you feel as though you're not in your body at all. When you see a car crash or a fire or a mugging from distance, it's almost as though you're sat in your dirty living room, watching on the television, waiting for it to unfold. You are simply a pair of eyes, taking in all the horror. A voyeur on the astral plane.

There is of course the implication of danger, but it's so removed from you personally, that you just take a backseat. You don't have to be involved, and if you stand still enough, you become invisible. Just like that, you're safe, bulletproof. You're an observer. The danger can't get to you. No risk, no pain, no responsibility and no fear. Just non-judgmental, passive observation.

And like a fool, you believe that delusion. Completely frozen, you are oblivious to any potential threat that is always just around the corner. There are consequences for actions and no deed, good or bad, goes unpunished. The truth is, that fire won't stop for anyone. The mugger might come for you next. You forget that thunder is just one member of a dangerous duo. In the trance, I stand clenched and unbreathing, waiting for the next cruel whip of thunder. I grit my teeth as I brace for the imminent blow.

I'm waiting for what feels like an eternity, but I don't dare unclench myself out of fear of being caught off guard. I wonder for how long I can maintain this state of tension before my teeth crack under the pressure, but there's no release. No catharsis.

BANG BANG BANG

Isn't that strange?

There's still no lightning.

I feel heat flush through my cheeks and suddenly I'm very much in the firing line of the storm. I'm no longer in the backseat, I'm at the wheel, on course for collision, and the brakes have been cut.

BANG BANG BANG

That doesn't sound like thunder. Was that my door? But how could it be?

Every hair on my body stands erect as my eyes fix on the door – the source of the 'thunder'. I'm now very aware that what I am afraid of can't in fact be a storm. What reason would I have to be afraid of a storm? You have to back your instincts; they don't lie after all. This fear could not be so intense over a bout of heavy weather. I'm safe in my house, nothing can get in. But, this banging, which is no longer distant and no longer impersonal, is at my front door. It's almost like it's calling for me. Of course, that can't be possible, no fool would be outside in this weather unless they wanted to be just another victim of the rain documented on the news. They'd be yet another poor soul emotionlessly listed off by the newsman, accompanied by a humiliating and gruesome image of a deformed and unrecognisable body reduced to a smouldering pile of viscera. Jesus, what am I even saying? Maybe I am going mad? I've been alone in this house for so long without contact from anyone; maybe I want someone to be at my door. If I can create memories, create different stories, maybe I can just make this visitor disappear? But no, I can't be imagining this. Far different from the booming crack of thunder which vibrates through your bones, this unrelenting banging ripples across the walls of the house. It's too different from the light and casual tapping of the rain. It's too precise, too perfect. It's cold and mechanical, robotic even.

It's unmistakable. Someone is knocking at my door. I'm frozen in fear now, even more so than before and I'm briefly thankful that there are no mirrors in my house as I would be equally as terrified at the pale and saucer eyed fool staring back at me. The only movement I can manage is a quick glimpse out the window.

There has been no movement outside except for the rain. The streetlamp shines no light on the situation. There are still no cars, just an empty road. There is only unflinching nothingness outside which makes the incessant assault on my door all the more confusing.

BANG BANG BANG

Machine-like, the intervals between each knock remain consistent. This metronomic timing has me flinching in tandem.

Who? Who? Who is it?

Every knock sends violent shivers down my spine, which in my stone like rigidity, threatens to shatter me into a million pieces. But despite this apprehension I can't help but think of the poor soul at my door. They must be in agony and desperation. Why else would they be knocking at the door of a stranger? Of course, I can't assume that everyone is as cowardly as me and perhaps interacting with another person isn't as unthinkable as I believe it to be.

Maybe I'm overreacting. That can't be right, though.

There is nobody else outside. I haven't seen a single soul for God knows how long. That must mean I'm right, and this person must be in danger…right?

Goodness, I need to stop stalling.

It doesn't take a genius to realise that now is the time for action instead of these questions, because if I don't hurry, they'll be dead. Do I really want this person's blood on my hands? It'll take an awful lot of rain to wash that off…

BANG BANG BANG

I have to let them in. What kind of monster would I be if I didn't? God, I am a coward. I am such a coward. I've been one my whole adult life, and maybe there's nothing wrong with that, after all, it's kept me alive to this day – but one thing I am not, is a monster.

The banging is deafening now and cannot be ignored. Each knock is a plea, begging for me to open up. I slowly and unsurely start towards the door.

I keep my eyes primed on the door, I haven't walked through the short corridor leading to my front door in God knows how long and I need to remain focused on what's important right now. It smells musty here like an old garage, dust and cobwebs galore.

As I reach out towards the handle, the banging stops, and all I can hear are the ambient licks of rain at the door.

My hand stays frozen above the door handle.

Why has it stopped? Is that the end of the ordeal? Can I go back to my sofa and resume my usual duties of sitting idle in front of the TV?

In this little break, I notice sweat gathering on my brow.

It's funny, not even two minutes ago I was completely unaware of my body. All that existed was the front door and whatever was on the other side, but now I feel my heart. I feel my lungs taking short, shallow hits of stale air. I can feel the sting of sweat in my eyes. I close them and grimace, but I can't bring myself to rub them. All my energy is focused on the door when I hear a voice.

"Please open up".

His voice is so clear. It feels like he's standing right behind me, whispering in my ear, or bizarrely, like he's in my head.

My God, can he see me?

My hand is still hovering over the handle. And it's shaking more than ever.

"Please…help me. Why won't you help me?".

I finally rub my eyes to end the stinging and a part of me hopes that when I reopen them, whatever is at my door will be gone; It's all in my head. Surely? But who am I kidding? wishful thinking never gets me anywhere.

Keeping my eyes shut I take in a deep breath and suck in as much air as possible while I attempt to steady my shaking hand on the cold brass of the doorhandle. Squeezing so tightly that my knuckles go white, I pull the doorhandle downwards.

My ears ring. I don't remember opening the door.

2

My eyes hurt so much. I don't know if it's the sweat pouring out of me or maybe flecks of rain have entered my home as the door stands wide open. But something is deeply irritating my eyes, and copious amounts of rubbing seems to be the only thing staving off the burning. Whatever impaired my vision has apparently deafened me too, for every sound from before is dampened by a high-pitched ringing. The rain is barely audible. I can't hear any breathing, nor can I hear anything coming out of my TV. Stranger still, the intense stuffiness of my house remains the same. I would've expected that with the door open, there would possibly be a gust of wind or a change in temperature, but it feels like I am standing in a vacuum. Now as I take jagged gulps of musty air, it's like somebody has pressed a pause button, and I'm just standing here bracing myself, waiting to see what stands before me.

It's only when I finally open my eyes, that the ringing stops. After a few seconds of cloudy shapes, the stinging also ceases, and the blurry mass forming before me begins to transform into a tall, harsh looking man.

He's staring right at me. His dark, deep-set eyes give nothing away as they stay firmly locked on me. Now unable to stand still, I squirm as I fail to maintain eye contact. My eyes dart uncontrollably from point to point, anywhere except at his. Without looking away from me, he half turns to the door and casually flings it shut.

"Well…aren't you gonna say hi?"

I'm no expert in the art of conversation, but I'm pretty

sure that's not how you're supposed to greet someone you don't know. Unable to determine whether his intentions are sinister or not, I can't help but dribble out a whimper of a response,

"Oh, sorry – hi."

Instantly, the man's expression softens, he probably feels pity for me. Isn't that weird? I have just let this stranger into my house, saving him from certain death, and he has automatically assumed a position of dominance. Am I really so passive that he already sees himself as the man in charge here? It's actually quite insulting. Who does he think he is to judge me so quickly? Despite that, I can't help but feel a sense of gratitude that he saw my confusion and demonstrated with a subtle smile and an unfurrowing of the brow, that maybe he is friendly.

"So, can I come in?"

His confidence only serves to stun me further into befuddlement. He is acting with a familiarity that I'd expect from someone I've known for years, but I don't think I've ever seen this man before in my life. He speaks with a cool arrogance about him and his woody, gravelly voice seems a mismatch with the smug expression he wears on his face. Then, as he proceeds to walk in before I can even respond, his thick, chapped lips twist into a smirk. Despite this however, he doesn't seem to be making these expressions with malice or condescension. Furthermore, every action he makes is without hesitation. Every step is deliberate, every movement is relaxed, and every look he gives is confident. It doesn't appear to me that any of this is calculated or sinister - It is absolutely baffling to me. And perhaps feeling a bit guilty after seeing my puzzled reaction, he wears an expression of sympathy, not dissimilar to one you'd expect from an adult speaking to a confused child.

Part of me doesn't want to be so accommodating to this stranger who doesn't appear to be nearly as desperate or panicked as I imagined he would be. Nevertheless, I find myself on autopilot as I blankly nod my head and passively mutter "yeah, sure, come on in." The weak and nervous chuckle following this statement betrays any kind of effort to attain a level of assertiveness in this exchange.

"You can sit down here if you want," I gesture toward my sofa, the only seat in my living room, "but be careful when you sit down, watch out for your leg." I point to the razor edge of the table rather feebly and then draw an imaginary line on my shin. I wonder if there was even any point in mentioning it, he's not an idiot. For God's sake, now he thinks that I make that stupid mistake when I sit down – in my own home no less! He knows not to scratch his leg on the table. A wave of relief briefly washes over me however as I remember that he can't see my scarred shins.

"Cheers mate!" The stranger is slow but comfortable as he glides over to the couch. I think about how that is my spot, the imprint of my body is cast into the dirty polyester. I've spent many, many lonely nights forming that imprint. I silently curse myself for so casually offering up something which, to me, has value. Then, in a swift and fluid motion as though he's done it a thousand times before, the stranger flings himself onto my sofa causing it to thump into the back wall. I flinch when it makes contact, but I don't say a thing. I await the apology which never arrives when I notice it feels like I am the guest in this man's house. Watching him rest a dirty boot onto my already grubby coffee table, I glance at his shoe, bemused by the gall of him, but I remain silent. Noticing my look, the stranger in an instance of what seems like genuine concern asks,

"Would you prefer I keep my feet off the table, or is that alright?"

"No, no don't worry about it. It's absolutely fine!"

God, I wish he hadn't asked if it was alright. It's not. But I suppose that was pretty good of him to check at least.

Once again, I can't help but despise myself first for the pathetic laugh that keeps exiting my mouth after every sentence, but also for my inability to stop blindly trying to please this stranger who is in my home. He nods warmly with an accommodating smile on his face. After which, we both enter an awkward silence, and I am, once again, unable to successfully keep eye contact with the stranger.

During this silence, which feels considerably longer than it probably is, I can't help but take note of his eyes. There's something about them I detest. Even though I am managing to avoid looking at them for too long, I can't help but notice that they're impossibly dark. They're completely expressionless. This blankness conveys neither malice or benevolence, but the complete lack of any kind of life or emotion in them only leaves me feeling as soulless as I believe this stranger must be. When able to keep eye contact for more than a second, all I can feel is a pit in my stomach and an overwhelming sensation of despair. Paired with his thick, protruding brow which sits on his eyes like a hood, casting dark shadows; there is an impression of emptiness or that he is wearing a mask. Any semblance of a soul I may have, is sucked into these two abysses beneath his brow. With the addition of the small smirk etched into the side of his face, there is more unease piled on top of the already strange atmosphere. Maybe I'm just not as good at reading people as I should be, but due to this, I am struggling to figure anything out about this man. He gives off nothing and it is deeply unsettling. I honestly wonder if he is having any thoughts at all.

"You're not much of a talker, are you?" The wry smile curls further up the side of his face.

"I'm sorry. I am a little bit shaken if I'm being honest. I wasn't expecting company." I try my best to match his volume and clarity in how he speaks, but all that I can muster is a low mumble and of course, that wretched laughter.

"Actually, if I'm being honest, I'm kind of confused. I mean, I wasn't expecting you to be so casual and comfortable in here – not that there's any problem of course!"

Suddenly, the smirk is gone, and he looks stone faced and serious, "I have no reason to believe you're not being honest, do I? Would you prefer I was all awkward and nervous like you? This is your house, isn't it? Come on. Sit down, relax," after a brief but jarring absence, that smirk returns to his face, and with it, his own patronising laughter. Naturally, his laugh bothers me too, it's like a funhouse mirror version of mine whereas instead of the nervous giggle I produce, he has pitched his to a comically high level, no doubt to make fun of me. Of course, I don't dare let him know of my disapproval.

"Yeah of course, I'm just gonna take a seat over here." I shuffle over to the window where I was standing before this stranger entered my home, and back up against the wall beside it. Feeling the rain gently tickle the wall, I slink down so my knees are pressed up against my chest and lock them in with my arms. Bowing my head towards my knees, I take a deep but subdued breath and hold it in my lungs for a couple seconds. Regaining some kind of control over myself, I exhale and attempt to engage the stranger.

"I've got to ask though – and obviously I'm relieved that you're ok of course – but what were you doing outside? Again…I mean no disrespect in asking that, but I'd have expected that – that you'd at least be a bit more shaken or something, given the weather and all? I mean, they said we're not supposed to be outdoors at all."

And now that I've said it aloud, it really dawns on me that this man is completely unscathed. That isn't to say he's without blemishes. Physically, he's a hard looking man. His features are large and blunt, like they've been broken and repaired countless times. He is littered with scars which have long since healed, but remain nonetheless as reminders of previous battles, he's also a large man. Now, I am by no means small myself, but this man looks so much bigger now he's sat in my sofa. He doesn't seem to dwarf me in size, in fact he can be no taller than me, but his demeanour and presence is far larger than mine. His body is cruel, strong and calloused, and even though he's sitting, he looks coiled and sturdy, like he could pounce at any moment. It would be of no surprise to me if he has in fact tussled with real demons from the murkiest depths of hell and has come out the other side stronger. But despite all these battle scars and signs of former injury, the complete lack of any fresh wounds or new damage is what shocks me. And while I was somewhat unable to maintain eye contact with this stranger when he entered my home, I can't help but wonder how I didn't notice beforehand that his clothes aren't even wet.

There is a reason why nobody is outside. There is a reason the news warns of the dangers of doing such a thing. There must also have been a reason why this man was roaming the streets. Was there a reason he knocked at my door?

"Firstly, nobody tells me what to do. So, whoever 'they' is, is of no interest to me. And secondly, it's gonna take a hell of a lot more than a bit of drizzle to take me down." And right on cue, he smirks. But this smirk is different to the one from before, it feels more direct. It seems targeted.

I'm starting to wonder whether him knocking at my door was random or not.

"Who are you?", I'm finally able to say with a bit of bass and strength. With the benefit of hindsight, I have a feeling that it may have been a mistake.

Like divine intervention, the sky above answers my question. Although I am unsure what the answer means. Finally lightning arrives alongside the now deafening thunder in a huge strike which feels as though it is shaking the house. Blinding flashes reveal the rain and desolation outside my window, and I'm frightened. Thankfully I am quick to remember it is safe inside here. That feeling is extremely short lived however, for staring vacantly at me is the stranger, apparently unable to hear my question and apparently unshaken by the storm attacking my home. Meanwhile my question echoes in my head like the dull thud of a hammer, only slightly dampened by the sound of thunder, but still knocking into my skull -

Who are you? Who are you? Who are you?

My stomach twists and turns inside me and I am flooded with feelings of pure sorrow. I don't know if it's the ferocity and intensity of the thunder and lightning outside, or if the stranger is willing these feelings into me, but I am overwhelmed by dread and helplessness.

Perhaps he is just trying to mock me with this silent response. He must've already gathered that I'm easily startled, but there is no hint of humour or light-heartedness coming from him. No glint in his eye to suggest any kind of warmth, in fact there isn't even any inkling of sinister intention. The stranger exudes nothing. There is no light behind his eyes. There is no sign of him stopping this eerie staring contest, he continues, without flinching. He's challenging me to a game of chicken, and he's winning. The storm persists with increasing volatility. I'm sure it'll crash through the walls if it continues at this rate.

An uncomfortable amount of time passes until I can't contain my fear and discomfort anymore, so I stand up. He's won the exchange, and I'm floundering like a fish caught on a hook. I attempt to back away, but the wall is behind me preventing my escape from this strange episode. Like a broken record repeating the same, usually innocent line, this awful scene and my own question replays distorted and disfigured, and I'm waiting for the needle scratch to send us both back to normality. Weak and helpless, I can only stand with my mouth agape, unable to produce words, wondering when this will end and what will happen when it eventually stops. Then, like he was in control of the weather this whole time, he smiles.

The lightning stops. So does the thunder. All that's left is the rain.

"You know who I am,"

"I do?"

"I'm a man who needs your help. Won't you help me?" And instead of the smirk which has become as predictable as my spinelessness, he switches back to the blank and glassy eyed stare he had when he entered. I can no longer hear the rain; I can only hear my own heartbeat and my stuffy nasal breathing. Both have reached an unsustainable speed and, in what I can assume is my body acting in self-defence, I switch onto autopilot. Before I can even think of answering him, and God knows I have no idea what to say to that question, the TV increases its own volume as it sometimes does, and the newsman interjects with some more of his 'wisdom',

"Due to the lethal nature of the weather, it is being advised by top health officials that regular handwashing and general upkeep of good hygiene will be crucial for staying safe during this period. The recommendation from the Institute of Civilian Health states that handwashing should occur every 20 minutes in order to prevent illness which may require one to leave their home. Furthermore, checks for mould should be carried out regularly and frequently. Preventative measures should be exercised, with the following recommendation coming from leading experts – sealant should be applied to ceilings and walls to prevent any rain getting into your home, and any black mould, or areas which used to be covered in mould, should be sprayed daily with anti mould spray - running water should also be used sparingly to prevent the growth of harmful black mould." The newsman's face hardens in typical performed seriousness and then he adds, "Additional and new information suggests that if symptoms such as runny nose, scratchy throat, or a reddening of the eyes are present, a remedy of bleach, hot water and honey in equal parts should be consumed every 15 minutes until symptoms subside."

This little newsflash is bookended with a formal but high energy jingle, such is the norm with these types of messages. What a load of nonsense, I'm expected to limit the use of running water, but I'm supposed to wash my hands every 20 minutes, and this incredible advice comes from 'leading experts', whoever they are! That being said, the newsman has been my saviour here – it's not the first time and probably won't be the last. The stranger doesn't need to be an immediate problem, this handwashing malarkey has bought me a few minutes of time to compose myself.

"I'll help you but first I have to wash my hands". I silently pray that he doesn't dismiss this conveniently timed request as a time-buying tactic, but judging by his blank face, it seems as though he didn't hear the TV anyway. He nods curtly as I dart out the room; I dare not to look at him or the black mould on my walls as I exit the living room.

Thank God for the news. This typifies the love-hate relationship we have. I don't know where they come up with the nonsense that they spew, but occasionally they come out with some gems of genuine wisdom. Thankfully I know what to listen to and what to block out entirely. And as stupid as that may sound, it can be a real lifesaver sometimes.

3

I naively hope the stranger doesn't notice my nervous and jittery movements as I bolt out of the living room. Leaving the stranger and the living room behind me, I barge into my filthy bathroom turning the faucet on as hard as it will go so that the water sprays all over my arms, shirt and floor. Scrubbing my hands furiously, I struggle to digest the reality of what has actually just happened, I turn the heat on the tap all the way up. It burns and stings the cuts around my fingertips but it's somewhat cleansing. Besides, I've heard the TV say that boiling water kills germs, so I soldier on knowing it's doing good. I think about what is good for me for a moment. I think about the stranger asking for my help, I think about the mould growing on the walls, I try to think about any relationships I've had in the past – it's all as painful as the water. Then, as the intensity and ferocity of this little episode reaches boiling point, I snatch my hands out from under the scalding water and turn the tap down so that it's just a gentle stream flowing out. Trying my best to contain any noise acknowledging the pain, I look up at the ceiling with my eyes closed. Upon letting out a sharp and loud breath, I grimace in order to keep tears from building up in my eyes. Mission accomplished.

I refocus on the wall in front of me. I can't help but fixate on a lighter square of wall above the sink. It's a noticeably paler shade of grey compared to the dull and filth laden wall around it. That's odd. There must have been a mirror there. And it must've been removed somewhat recently for it to be less scum laden than the rest of the wall. So, now I find myself wondering why there is no mirror above the sink. Then, as quickly as that thought enters my head, the answer is revealed. It's so obvious to me, that I can't help but laugh at my own ignorance. And once again, I am presented with the opportunity to test my admittedly patchy memory.

It's worth noting that the absence of a mirror in my bathroom is not a coincidence and it's certainly not a stylistic choice, in fact there are no mirrors in my home. For longer than I care to admit, I've opposed and have maybe even been fearful of seeing my own face. Perhaps it's self-hatred, and it might be fair to say that I'm occasionally harsh about my capabilities, both physically and mentally. But it might also be accurate to suggest that it is for reasons of arrogance that I am unable to look at myself. I am not a handsome man, nor am I an avid smiler. I am not a doer of good deeds, nor am I particularly skilled at anything manual or intellectual, honestly, I am nothing more than a lowly bottom feeder – and that in itself is a generous summation. Even a parasite takes the necessary risk of being exterminated by a larger and more powerful creature in order to survive, whereas I am quite content feeding off the rotting garbage that others higher up on the food chain so carelessly throw to the wayside. In doing nothing, I remain safe. That is who I am, and I have accepted that this is my place in life, so it is not as though this fear is born completely from delusion.

Although, it's probably far more likely that nobody ever really sees me. The notion that people who don't know me would ever look twice or would even care is laughable. Therefore, this fear or unease about seeing myself is not just ridiculous, but it could only really be seen as narcissistic. Perhaps I only see myself? How self-indulgent. Irrespective of where this irrational behaviour originated, it remains true that I take great discomfort in having to see myself. It's something I have avoided for a long, long time.

And despite it becoming increasingly difficult to remember anything from my past with much clarity, there is one memory which is seared into my brain as though it was burned with an iron brand. So, while I should probably be more worried than I currently am about my inability to even remember my own father's face, I can take solace in the fact that this memory (at least for now) will always be my own. It should also be noted that this isn't an epic or emotional story, but often times, something that is greatly significant to one person, is completely uninteresting to another, and maybe my inability to understand the motives or feelings of other people is a small but tangible link I share with them when they in turn fail to understand me. When I remember this incident there isn't necessarily a beginning, middle and an end. I feel like most memories don't really follow that structure. You simply remember key points and the intense feelings they evoke, and you piece them together based on that. Therefore, I cannot claim that my recount of this incident is one hundred percent accurate, but it's one of the few things that stands out to me as a notable event in my life, for whatever reason that may be. One thing I can guarantee is that this memory is particularly painful for me, and hey - if pain isn't the best teacher, then I don't know what is.

The intricate details are irrelevant, but I can certainly remember the emotions I felt. The extreme highs and the extreme lows. I can't remember what I was wearing. I can't remember where I was going. But I do recall that I was content, and I was at peace.

There were lots of people present, but no discernible or notable ones in particular. The sound of hundreds, maybe thousands, of voices bouncing off the walls and then being compressed together gave the impression that instead of a group of individuals, they were one being - one hive mind. This loud rabble of mindless drones, none of whom would ever be able to understand me, and who I myself would never be able to truly know, were nothing but a comforting white noise. That was their purpose. I can't even pretend that I can begin to understand their own thoughts, wants, hopes and dreams, because to me, they were playing the role of background character. I don't doubt that they might be complex individuals in their own right, but how does that serve me? They were cattle. That's it and I was surrounded by them, like a protective wall - a luxury I took for granted, although I am still uncertain as to whether they were friends, colleagues, or even schoolmates, in fact I can't really recall their faces. There is only one I can remember because she was the most beautiful girl I had ever seen. I think her name was Sarah. Sadly, that's pretty much all I can recall about her. I can't remember her voice, how I knew her, or even who she was. I can't even be certain that her name was Sarah. Despite that, I like to believe that she was my girlfriend, and I like to imagine she had the most sweet and soulful voice that evoked joy like the song of an angel. That usually just makes the memory more painful though.

Furthermore, I can only remember her with two facial expressions, my mysterious Janus. One of which was a warm and broad smile, with full lips and large chestnut eyes. Her petite, button nose was the central point that her other features closely neighboured. Her rich olive skin and her little round face was the canvas upon which these delicate features were painted. She had a real girl next door sort of look, But I don't expect that she ever noticed I was her neighbour. The second was a look of sheer, crippling terror. All the colour and fragility had flushed from her cheeks leaving her hollow and ugly. Unsurprisingly that is the look I revisit most.

There we were in this shopping mall, and looking up, there were rows and rows of floors to mindlessly amble and have meaningless interactions and spend money. It was probably what most people would describe as the setting for a perfectly normal and innocent day out. I believe this was my usual hangout spot and the gentle braying of families and other groups of people shuffling along like sheep was quite relaxing. Gargantuan cups of coffee, the smell of synthetic sugars and sickly-sweet optimism was rife in this little snapshot of faux happiness. The centrepiece of this circus however was an ornate, marble fountain which couldn't have looked more out of place in this hell hole. This magnificent work of art standing amongst Primark and Greggs, which would've been more at home in a museum than in this soulless place, was dying a slow and quiet death, drowning in a sea of tracksuits and trainers. It was seemingly invisible to everyone.

Well - almost everyone.

Back then I was able to fake smile to other people and wear a pleasant façade, but I only felt at true peace when I'd see this fountain. I smiled at the people surrounding me, but the real subject of my attention was this marble mausoleum of culture. Powerful yet carefully carved figures of angels, heroes of old and people long dead were semi submerged in a cloudy pool of dark green water. It always astonished me how this wonderful fountain, which had probably seen so much in its long and distinguished life, had ended up in this place. It was destined to fade away into nothingness, it would never be appreciated in a place like this.

I can see it clear as day, although in the memory whenever I speak, all I can hear or recall is muffled feedback, but never any words. I must be speaking though; everyone is looking at me. Anything I say is simply absorbed by the white noise of the crowd. The faces of those around me are still bright and almost cartoonish as they nod and react to me with warmth and interest, even though I have no idea what it is I am saying. Their smiles are too wide, and their eyes are maniacal. All the attention was on me, and it felt wonderful, but it also feels strange. It feels fabricated. And even though people were smiling at me, apparently due to something witty and insightful that I said, I can't help but keep my focus on that fountain. The fountain is the only thing I can see so clearly. That, and the seemingly endless tiers of this shopping mall. And even though I was stood on the ground floor, I get constant flashes of the mall from different perspectives - one moment I'm on the ground floor, the next I'm looking down from the upper ring of the mall, staring into the gaping pit below me.

The more I think about the fountain, the more I can remember the magnetism of it. It had this immense gravitational pull, but I also remember not putting up much of a fight as it drew me towards it. I felt like it only had eyes for me because nobody else seemed to be affected by it. And either looking down, or looking directly in front of me, all I could hear was the soothing buzz of the crowd around me. I was a lamb being herded towards the abattoir, very much aware of some unseen danger looming ahead, but still unconcerned and optimistic – I was simply enjoying the ride. Unbothered by this conveyer belt I found myself on, just enchanted by the destination. This situation was dizzying and confusing, and much like a picture show being played on a loop, way too fast to take in each image with any clarity, I am shown the fountain, the levels of the mall, Sarah and her smile, and then the fountain again, the tiers of the mall, and Sarah again. It hurts my head reliving it, but it's a necessary pain. Good pain. I enjoy it while I can, as it's proof that I'm still alive. I'm still here. Very subtly, the speed of the picture show increases. So subtly, in fact, that I can barely notice it, likewise, the sound of the people around me pick up the volume.

This continues until the picture show is almost at a dizzying blur, and I can only vaguely make out the images as I slowly and mindlessly make my way towards the fountain. On repeat, the fountain, the tiers of the mall and the escalators, Sarah, her smile, they continue to assault me. This flickering loop, which somehow is the only way I can remember this incident, persists. The unrelenting nature of this little episode paired with a gradual increase in speed and volume only amplifies the sense of impending dread I was feeling. The growing speed all seems to be leading towards a crash of some sort, I begin to tense in anticipation that something catastrophic is about to occur.

And right on cue, amongst the harmless images of the shopping centre, Sarah, and the fountain, there is a mysterious intrusion.

Like subliminal messaging planted into old advertisements, scattered on only a couple frames of film, I begin to notice an abnormality. I almost don't notice it at all at first. But as these images whizz around my head while I walk towards the fountain, I recognise the image as a man on a ledge. And while the other images were all from my perspective where I was stood, this view is extremely tight to the man, as though I were stood right behind him.

the man on the ledge features more prominently the closer I get to the fountain, almost as though the fountain itself is summoning him. The ledge he is stood on looks familiar, but I'm not quite sure why.

As I near the fountain, the buzz of the shoppers is now much higher than a low din, it's incrementally increasing in volume. I hadn't initially noticed it getting louder, but now I find myself wincing at its intensity more than before. I wait for someone bolder than me to address this noise; everyone is screaming!

There he is again! The man on the ledge, his back towards me, his hands gripping the rail in front of him so firmly.

It's the top ring of the mall. I recognise it now.

The closer I get to the fountain, the closer I get to the man. His shoulders are bowed, and his head hangs so low it appears as though he is headless.

The noise is deafening now, it roars thunderously like it disapproves of what I am seeing.

What was once a low rumble is now a mind splitting storm, and my vision is a blur as I finally reach the fountain.

For a second, the picture show stops, and I only see the man. I can't see his face at all, but I can see his slouched posture. His rounded shoulders. And maybe I'm not a people person, and I don't read them very well, but it's a posture I recognise as that of the hopeless man. That's how I remember it anyway. He's looking down into the shopping centre, down into those rings like the circles of hell.

And as I get nearer and nearer, I can see his shoulders gently bouncing up and down. If it was quieter, I would know for sure whether he is sobbing or laughing. I wasn't sure of anything, but I felt I had to act before it was too late.

The last thing I observe of this man is my own outstretched hand reaching for him.

Then I see Sarah's face and she isn't smiling anymore. She looks like she's seen a ghost.

I'm stood at the fountain now, and the rapid whirlwind of the picture show has lulled until I'm standing right next to the ledge, peering down at the pool of fetid liquid.

Finally, there is tranquillity. The roar of the crowd has hushed, and I find myself in a trance as I gaze into the murky green water. I lock eyes with my reflection which is misshapen by gentle rippling. I don't recognise the face in the water, but it looks familiar. It must be mine.

It's hideous.

The stinking water is everywhere as the reflection consumes me. The surprising cold sends me into shock and suddenly the memory is once again foggy. Wondering what caused this immense splash, I look around to see the reactions of everyone else.

Everyone is just staring at me – but differently this time.

And again, I am attacked by the offensive sound of the high-pitched ringing.

There were only two others who I vaguely recognised. Sarah was there with that terrible look on her face, the only other expression she had. Her eyes were inhumanly large but drained of life at the same time. The look she gave me was one of incredible fear but also one of judgement as though I was some kind of monster. She was screaming something, but all I could hear was the ringing feedback, so naturally I turned away from her rather than revel in the discomfort. Besides, she didn't look very beautiful like this.

Of course, I was also present in the literal sense, but I feel like my mind was miles away. I didn't want to be anywhere near this situation. I felt like I was having an outer body experience. I could feel the burn of Sarah's eyes as I stood in front of the fountain. This kind of attention was nowhere near as enjoyable as the adoration I was receiving before. It was all deeply unsettling.

The only other person there was someone I didn't recognise until I looked over the ledge of the fountain. It was at that moment where I saw what had caused the commotion, and I realise that the people probably weren't looking at me.

It was the man from the top of the shopping mall. Upon seeing his face and his dark, glassy eyes, and his twisted body half submerged in the remaining green water, I was overwhelmed with an odd combination of embarrassment, shame and despair. I remember thinking we looked quite similar, but that might have been because we were both, in that moment, deeply alone, deeply lost and would rather have been somewhere else.

It felt good to share that feeling with him. Standing over him, I attempted to contort my body into the same position as his, but I couldn't force my body to bend into those unnatural shapes no matter how hard I tried. Upon getting very uncomfortable staring at him I became unsure what to do with my body. My hands felt awkward hanging by my side, and I remember lowering them into my pockets. My clothes were bone dry. It was then that I was assaulted by a terrible, dizzying sensation.

Unable to think of the right thing to say, I was suddenly draped in an uncomfortable warmth pouring over the surface of my skin. The heat in my cheeks also brought about tears in my eyes, although I am not much of a crier, so it must've been water from the fountain. I wanted to help, but I was too afraid to move, I was too crippled to take action. Shivering and confused in what should have been wet clothes, I opened my mouth to speak, but there was nothing I could say – nothing I could offer. Thankfully, the man was able to speak with the little life he had left in him. His rasping, breathless words reminded me more of a dying animal than a living, breathing human being – a living breathing human being who very likely had hopes and dreams, and maybe even loved ones. It doesn't matter anyway, because I could barely hear him above the ringing, and he wasn't going to be living or breathing for much longer,

"Please help me. Why won't you help me?"

And as faint as it was, the voice sounded so familiar, and those words knocked the wind out of me.

I looked back over to Sarah, her face still frozen in terror, as the trickling sound of the fountain is drowned out by the rain.

4

I feel fragile and limp as I stare at my shaking hands. Revisiting my past, what little of it I remember, is proving to be a painful ordeal. But as I've already said, the intensity of the emotion can be exciting, albeit a little draining. This dazed weightlessness, if I can call it that, is not dissimilar to the tipsiness you feel after having a couple of drinks. And while I'm certainly not an alcoholic, I find this feeling to be just as addictive as any drug, and I'm in no rush to untether myself from this particular addiction. But rather than address that unhealthy admission by plunging into the depths of self-pity, I must first deal with this stranger in my living room. The flow of time can be so misleading and while it has only felt like a couple of minutes reliving my memory, my bearings are all over the place and for all I know, years could have passed since I have been in the bathroom! In all honesty, I kind of hope that dreaded guest of mine has either left my home, or that he has died of starvation. I'm not picky though, both are acceptable outcomes to me.

As I re-enter the living room however, half expecting – and half hoping - to be met with the emaciated remains of the stranger laying on the floor with his arms splayed by his side and his jaw limply hanging open, I am disappointed to see him still comfortably sat on the sofa, watching me walk over to my designated spot by the window. Smirk, fixed on his face, eyes honed in on me like a blowtorch, the "normal" proceedings have resumed. I haven't even had time to reach the wall I had been sitting against before he remarks,

"Nice of you to join us!"

That smug prick. Every action of his infuriates me, and while I am still very much incapable of even locking eyes with him, the feeling of hatred I have is certainly outweighing the genuine concern I initially felt. I can only hope that the anger bubbling up inside of me will recede soon, because I sure as hell will not have the courage to voice these issues with him. Despite all this, I flash him a little, tight-lipped smile, and a squinting of the eyes. I feel this is a sufficient response to his sarcastic little quip rather than vocalising my disapproval.

"Are your hands nice and clean now? Will you finally be able to help me?"

"Yeah — sorry about that, sometimes I get a little stressed and, I don't know, washing my hands calms me down for some reason" I reply, ducking his second question.

"Well, I had no intention of causing you any distress, I promise you that," his brow hardens over his eyes as he says this, and his smirk has a sinister air about it. He also didn't question my lie about washing my hands — or maybe he genuinely didn't hear the newsflash earlier.

"No, I'm sure you didn't. You don't seem like that sort of bloke," I'm cautious and careful to avoid provoking the stranger into another staring contest. The imminent danger that I felt last time was nigh unbearable, and if I have to tiptoe around him to prevent that, so be it. I decide that it would probably be just the right level of assertiveness — and safety — to tread carefully if I want to make it out of this encounter unscathed.

"You mentioned earlier that you need my help. With all due respect, you seem to be doing pretty well on your own, a lot better than me in fact. I'm not too sure what sort of support I could offer to you, unless there's anything you need in here?"

"I wouldn't put yourself down so much if I were you. You aren't doing nearly as badly as you might think, after all you're still alive, aren't you? I can't say it's particularly cosy in this place, but it's yours at least. It's your own little castle, and I suppose whatever situation you've got going on in here is probably safer than outside. Otherwise, you wouldn't be cooped up in here, right?" Why am I tense around this guy? Maybe he isn't so bad after all, and once again my poor judgement and understanding of people has misled me. He does seem to be pretty understanding of my situation, and hell, he's even making excuses on my behalf. Perhaps I'm just being paranoid. "With that being said, I do need your help. I need your help because I've been watching you. You might think nobody sees you, but I see you. I know you. And I need you to help me."

I open my mouth to react, but silence elucidates my thoughts more eloquently. I am physically unable to conjure the words to convey how I feel at this little revelation. How the hell has he been watching me? All this time I've been standing by that window looking out, it didn't dawn on me that other people could see in. God, I really need to invest in some blinds. But how much has he seen? For how long has he been watching? What is it he needs me to do? And furthermore, where was he? There is nobody outside. It is completely empty out there. If it weren't for the news channel, I'd have good reason to believe that the world had ended, and that these four walls were the only remaining fragments of society. Given the lack of change of the landscape outside, what I see on the window could very well be a painting! So where has this stranger been hiding? Where has he come from? From where has he been watching me? These thoughts whizz around my head as I attempt to keep a lid on the anger and panic bubbling inside of me.

"Listen, I can see you're panicking. But there's nothing to be worried—"

"Nothing to be worried about! Are you crazy? Do you really expect me to just be ok with the fact that you've been spying on me? How did you think I would react? And what's more, you've come into my home and – and – now you expect complete compliance from me. You must be out of your fucking mind! I – I don't know how else I would respond. You obviously don't know me at all!"

"Listen. I know it's a lot for you to hear and a lot to take in. Your reaction is completely natural. It's expected. But I do need your help. So please just take a moment and breathe." Though he can be no older than me, his tone is parental and authoritative. More impressive still, he isn't crossing the line into being condescending and I can feel the hate I had for this man simmer down with each word. We are two grown men sat in this room but this stranger, even after my brief outburst, hasn't raised his voice. His ability to maintain this level of composure is something I could only dream of. Once again, I breathe in deep and slow, holding the breath in my lungs, hoping it'll stop the storm brewing in my head. After having slipped, I am able to refocus myself. I'm able to reconnect with the rainfall on the back of the wall. My thumping heartbeat manages to regain a normal rhythm on the offbeat of the rain, and as I feel its tickle, the stress is washed away, but so is the temporary urge to fight. Defeated, and with the fire inside me dwindling by the second, I look in the stranger's horrible eyes,

"What do you need me to do?"

As I say this, I am able to maintain eye contact with him, and this feels like a huge victory. He even looks more human than before. His features almost completely transform before me. They have softened considerably, and the thick ridge above his eyes has risen up to reveal two black pearls. What were previously soulless are suddenly filled with sadness, and for the first time he appears to be genuinely vulnerable, and I can actually share his pain in a moment of unity. This union feels more like a reunion as he looks rather familiar now, and for a moment, it almost feels like I recognise him.

But that slip of his mask is extremely brief. Nearly as soon as it appears, it is replaced by a coldness that causes me to shiver. The fatherly warmth has vanished, and the glistening black pearls have become dead lumps of coal. His voice becomes cold and mechanical, crunching like the gears of an old car.

"I need you to come outside with me. I need you to stand with me in the rain." His words are gruff and to the point. They cut through the sound of the storm like a hot knife.

"What?"

He stares at me, his face unchanging, as though he hasn't heard my remark, or maybe he did hear, and he simply doesn't care about what I have to say. I contemplate repeating myself but as I open my mouth to do so, I find that I am unable to speak.

Focused and unrelenting, he keeps his steely glare on me, and the aching feeling of being punched in the gut returns.

I'm squirming and writhing under the weight of his stare, and the shrill ringing in my ears vibrates around my head, making it throb until I'm sure that my skull will crack. I rise to my feet as I cannot stay seated or in one position. Now in a state of hyper alertness, my eyes dart frantically around the room to avoid being in contact with his, and I am startled when a shock of thunder ends the ringing I hear in my ears. Still looking around with what I can only assume is an air of derangement in my eyes, I notice that the stranger, with his enormous presence, is still firmly rooted in one spot.

I imagine lunging at him. He thinks I'm a wimp, so what if I take him by surprise, hurling my fists wildly in a flurry of rage, each one an atomic blast pounding his skull repeatedly, only stopping once his face is nothing more than a lumpy pile of raw, red flesh. But I shake myself out of that little fantasy. The reality is much grimmer than my imagination.

The rain slaps the window and I turn my back to the

stranger, who's still seated in my couch, and refocus my attention outside instead. The rain applauds me for returning my gaze towards it and I sigh a breath of gratitude. So long as it's raining, I won't have to go outside. I'm safe in here.

"How can something as peaceful as water be so dangerous" I say quietly to myself, keeping my back facing the stranger, "What you're asking is unthinkable". I take his silence as agreement, "And not only is it unthinkable, but I don't understand what favour I'll be doing for you by going outside and dying". I sniff as I say this, but my nose isn't particularly runny.

More silence, but I'm more interested in the rain than anything this stranger has to say anyway. Besides, it's cathartic getting this all off my chest, and it's a lot easier to do it when I don't have to look him in the eyes.

"And another thing", this feels so good, this must be what confidence feels like. It's vaguely familiar, like a friend you fell out with and haven't spoken to in years. It's good to be reacquainted, but it's a little awkward and forced. "What good am I to anyone if I'm dead?" I feel joy as I say this, like a weight has been lifted off my shoulders, like I can finally move freely, and my lips quiver as my mouth takes on the unfamiliar shape of a smile. It's a foreign experience having the thrill of the emotion take control of me. As I do this, I feel hot globs of liquid pooling in the corners of my eyes, and they eventually spread across like a film, distorting my view and causing it to pulsate and ripple. I wipe the hot thick tears building up in my eyes as I sniff, confused as to why my body is contradicting my thoughts.

The stranger can only reply with a raised eyebrow. He actually looks as confused as I am, and I can see the thoughts whizzing around his head, his face being the better conveyor of his words right now. I can almost hear him with muted breaths and half uttered vowels, as he attempts to work out how my answer related to his question. Or maybe he's just confused by the dissonance between my emotions and my words.

He then looks at me with sadness again. It's clear that he pities me, but I have no idea why. I'm the one who's in control, does he not understand the dynamic here? I'm in charge of this exchange. He shakes his head and looks down in what looks like a moment of realisation. Whatever he's realised has got him pretty upset, however. What a fool. The newsman on the TV mentions something about 'the calm before the storm' and once again warns not to leave the house.

There's a roaring crack of thunder, then, much like an old oak tree in a crowded forest falling to the ground, ripping up earth and leaves with its roots, preparing to destroy everything in its wake; the stranger rises from my couch and begins walking towards me.

As this hulking presence slowly trudges my way - his steps seemingly in sync with every few taps of rain - all the so-called confidence I felt before immediately flushes out of me.

Now in a state of hyper vigilance, time has seemingly slowed down which gives me a moment to wonder whether he read my mind when I thought him a fool, and what it is he wants. I consider the idea of attacking him, but retreat seems like a more successful and realistic option, even though I wouldn't know where to retreat to. What seemed, only a few hours ago, like a haven now feels like a zoo enclosure; I'm trapped in this cage with a predator and it's feeding time. He doesn't say a word as he nears me, which only adds to the terror.

With an unrelenting emotionless stare, and bloodshot eyes encasing his oil black iris, he resembles an unfathomable force of nature more than a fellow man who needs my help.

Without words, warning, or any inkling as to what his intentions are, I make a dash for the door to the bathroom.

He follows me there, slowly of course, but inevitably,

without stopping. He reaches out to me with one of his thick arms, hand open and fingers spread.

I can only stand shivering, my feet rooted to the spot, wishing that time itself would freeze so I don't have to face what I know is coming.

One of his giant paws, armoured with callouses, lingers ominously beside my neck, I watch out the side of my eyes as it hovers there. I am briefly unable to turn my head.

I close my eyes, denying the tears I feel pouring down my face, and try to hear the rain, try to be anywhere else.

Then I feel his hand land heavily on my shoulder. Its warmth and firmness snap me back into the room. So firm, in fact that I stop shivering. I open my eyes again and he's only a foot in front of me. He isn't smiling, but his entire demeanour has changed. His menacing look has been replaced by one of sincerity and sympathy.

Something's off. He seems – concerned.

His hand grips my shoulder and gives it a little shake as he says very quietly, "You need to calm down, ok."

"What is going on here?"

"Well, it's pretty obvious, isn't it? It's very clear you've painted me as some kind of bad guy here, but I'm not who you seem to think I am," I bite my tongue so as not to ask who this man is. The terror from before is still very much fresh in my memory. "You aren't as mysterious as you believe yourself to be, everything you're thinking is written across your face and as much as I'm sure you'd prefer me to be as panicked and awkward as you are, that isn't who I am," it's so strange, can he sense my fear of that question? He seems to be steering the conversation towards that which I dare not ask again, naturally I refuse to budge, even when he says," I know who I am. Do you?"

"Do I know who I am? Well…yeah, sure. Of course, I

do…why?"

"Something is eating away at you, and I wonder if you even know what it is, and why it's affecting you this way? You're angry at me. You're angry at yourself. Why do you think that is?"

"I have no idea what you're talking about, and with all due respect, I'd prefer you to spare me the therapist talk." That was a mistake from me. I replied far too quickly.

He takes his heavy hand off my shoulder and points at the window, "you won't have any kind of peace out there until you quell whatever turbulence you have living inside your own head. If you don't – it will destroy you. I told you already – I know you. But you need to be honest with yourself, and in order for you to help me, you need to let me help you. I mean what use are you to anyone if you can't even help yourself?"

I sniffle. There must be a chill in here somewhere because I'm starting to feel ill, and my eyes are wet and sore. Perhaps the rain is finally seeping through the walls.

"What do you want me to say?" I feel completely helpless. "You say you already know me, so what more do you want? It doesn't matter what I say, does it? You've already made up your mind and there's nothing I can do to change that perception." The stranger has won. And in victory he stares me down with a grave look on his face. Then he pauses. Maybe for dramatic effect, or maybe he doesn't pause at all, and I'm just imagining it because, deep down, I know what he's going to say next. My pessimism is, once again, serving as a detrimental sixth sense and all I want is to avoid or prevent him from asking a certain question.

"I want you to tell me what happened that day."

"What - what do you mean?"

"I want you to tell me what happened at the fountain."

5

It's odd because I revisit the events of that day so frequently, but the more I try and think about what happened, the harder it is to remember any clear details. Each visit somehow muddies my already chequered account of what transpired. Maybe it's my mind's way of protecting me, but from what? Honestly, I don't even know why I suggested that. I hate that saying. It's a copout used to prevent people from questioning the real issue at hand. What could my mind be 'protecting' me from exactly? Every miserable moment in this house should serve as evidence that my mind is actively trying to attack me. I really don't know. What little I can remember is hazy at best.

I remember the man standing on the ledge, and then I remember him in the fountain. That's all…I think.

No. I also remember Sandra - or was her name Sally?

Well, what is important is that I remember her face anyway. It must be important, right? Why else would that be the only thing I remember? Maybe my mind is protecting me from something. The real question is what is it protecting me from? My own thoughts, maybe? Then again, how can I claim 'my mind' is protecting me from my thoughts when I am in fact painfully conscious of my own thoughts and feelings – I am my thoughts and feelings! How could I protect myself from myself? That would just be a lazy conclusion to come to. Besides, what harm could I possibly do to myself? What a stupid thing to say. If I'm aware that I am 'protecting' myself from myself, my being conscious of said protection surely nullifies any shielding from damage I may or may not be trying to achieve.

It doesn't really matter anyway, because I feel that my focus is misplaced. That may even be intentional. But rather than being concerned by my failing memory, the deterioration of which I am almost sure of; the majority of my energy is focused on the stranger.

How did he know about the fountain?

And, while I can't be absolutely sure that I've never seen him before, there is definitely something familiar about him, and maybe it's likely that I had bumped into him at some point in the past – long before I stopped leaving my home.

I suppose, he does claim to know me. I can't make such a claim about him, and as he has already implied, I probably can't make that claim about myself. It's also not something I want to address. Ignorance, in this case, is bliss.

But what am I thinking? Why am I trying to rationalise this stranger's words? This is a mad man who has admitted to stalking me, and for how long, I have no idea. Not only that, but he has also forced his way into my home and has demanded that I leave, probably so that I can face some kind of execution.

I'm not sure that I want to know, but I do feel that for my own safety, I probably should have some idea as to how he knows about that day at the fountain and for how long he has been 'watching' me. Whatever I do next, it would be wise to do so quickly, because I'm not sure I can just stand in silence, staring at the bridge of his hideous nose for too much longer.

He did ask me a question after all.

"I'm, sorry. What was that?" He waits after I say this, I assume for dramatic effect to telegraph his frustration and then he replies.

"What do you remember happening at the fountain that day?" There is a noticeable effort to remain emotionless as he grunts this, but his audible breathing betrays any pretence of calmness he is trying to promote. As he speaks, his words sound irregular and unbalanced, augmented by his accelerated breathing. I suppose he'll just have to wait, the impatient bastard.

And, once again, even though I can't remember the day all that clearly, that very question makes me feel sick. Sweat seeps out of my forehead as I feel my heart rate accelerate. I swear that I can hear it beating.

It's so stuffy in here. When did it get so humid? I attempt to lower my voice to veil the uncontrolled emotion escaping me. "How do you know me? I don't know you." And once again his breathing gets louder, he snorts and sniffs,

"You continue to sidestep my question. I am being incredibly patient here, but if you insist upon being evasive, I will have to try a more direct approach. Don't force my hand." I think he might be at breaking point, and now more than ever I feel in danger.

"No! You're right – and I'm sorry. I wasn't trying to avoid the question, I promise. I – I'm still thrown from your comment before. I know you're being patient, and very reasonable too, but my memory really is failing me these days, come on mate, it's not too unfair of me to ask where you know me from - if that's alright". I remain uncertain as to what is and isn't acceptable to say. This only makes me feel worse when I can see the anger boiling up inside the stranger. Each misstep is another sharp jab of the finger into the beast, it's only a matter of time before the beast retaliates.

Perhaps somebody more socially apt would be able to recognise when what they're saying is whipping somebody else into a frenzy. A better man would take control not only of the situation, but of himself. As natural as breathing, he would sense and assess what you should or shouldn't say to someone and then would be able to steer the conversation around such roadblocks and consequently, he would avoid catastrophe.

Unfortunately, I have not had such a model to sculpt myself

into. Even my own imaginings of the paragon of manhood are skewed by my self-loathing, and any awareness of my ineptitude does nothing to aid me, instead it only heightens the lingering and inevitable feelings of doubt which lurk silently over my shoulder. Always watching and waiting for the fall. Therefore, any ideal of how I should behave is usually just the inverse of how I see myself. As long as I can remember, that's always been the rule.

"If you don't recognise me then it will be very difficult for me to help you. In fact, it might already be too late."

"Too late? Too late for what?"

"Enough!" The thunder and lightning springs to life again as the stranger roars at me. He's breathing slowly but deeply, and I can hear his breath shaking as his massive shoulders bob up and down. "Now as much as you think hiding from my questions will keep you safe, you are only sentencing yourself to a much heftier punishment than the one you are currently serving. A good man died that day, and I'm not going to allow you to bullshit your way out of facing justice."

Did I hear that right?

"Justice?" What is this man suggesting? What does he think he knows about me?

"I won't ask you again. What happened at the fountain? I need to hear you say it. What did you do at the fountain?"

And instead of questioning these wild implications, which are clearly nonsensical, I can't keep prevaricating.

I will tell him everything I know. The thunder quietens down so that there is nothing to interrupt me. Defeated, I look down and nod my head gently in the sofa's direction, ushering the stranger to sit down in a less intimidating position. I watch as he scrapes his leg on the corner of the coffee table on his way to the couch – he winces. Serves him right, the prick. Again, he dumps himself heavily onto the sofa while rubbing his leg and tightening his lips, obviously trying to conceal the pain.

I of course take this opportunity to return to my spot by the window – it's still raining, thank God.

"I'm being completely honest when I say that my memory of that day is hazy. I promise you that!" I pause to let him take in my performed sincerity, but he doesn't acknowledge it. Instead, he just leers at me, his forearms resting on his knees and his hands clasped.

I continue uninterrupted, "I'm assuming you were at the shopping centre that day, so I'll spare you the details, but one thing of note was that it wasn't raining back then. I can remember that much, at least. I was with friends, but the only person who stood out to me was my girlfriend."

"What is your girlfriend's name?"

"Well, I'm not with her anymore, but her name was—" Jesus Christ! What the hell was her name? It definitely began with an 'S', or was it an 'F'? Oh God, that's it! "Sophie! Her name was Sophie," I think that's right.

"Sophie? OK. Then what happened?" He looks almost bored of what I'm saying, or maybe he's fed up. That would make two of us, and I can't say I blame him, it's not a particularly interesting story and I have no intention of sugar coating anything or performing some kind of theatre for this brute. I will simply tell him what I know and what I want him to hear. That's all he needs to know.

"Well, Sophie and I had gone to the shopping centre to hang out with our friends. I think it was something we used to do quite a lot. You see, back then, it was perfectly safe to leave your house."

"I'm well aware – continue."

"We were stood around the fountain when it happened." The mere mention of the incident causes the sky to growl from outside again. It was a moody and disapproving growl; it seems that the thunder and lightning also doesn't want me to tell this story. The stranger, however, is either uninterested or unaware of the noise. I wonder if he can even hear it. Nevertheless, I continue,

"I was enchanted by this fountain. To the point that I wasn't even listening to anything anyone else was saying. Everybody's voice had blended into one, and it was just me and the fountain."

"What was so special about this fountain then?"

"Well, that's the thing. There was nothing particularly special about it. I'd tell myself that it was some beautiful and ornate piece of artwork, lost in a foreign time and a foreign land. I'd imagine that it had this rich history and that it was ultimately created with love and care, with a clear vision as to what message it would tell the world, and what people it would inspire. It was always a mystery to me why nobody else seemed to give it the time of day. And, it's only now I'm saying it out loud, and I can look back with retrospective clarity, I realise it's far more likely that it was just a cheap imitation of something real. A copy. I doubt it actually had any history of its own, I doubt it had a creator with a vision or a soul, I doubt it even had any other admirers. In fact, I know it didn't have any other admirers. It probably had no purpose at all, it was there to simply exist, a placeholder put there to collect litter. And yet, whenever I remember it, it has a certain glow around it. It radiates a warmth which thaws the ice which had seemingly grown all around and allows me to move freely. The frostiness of everyone else's demeanour is powerless when I near that fountain. Its aura never failed to pull me in, and I genuinely believe that the fountain's lack of any discernible beauty was probably what drew me to it most. It was completely average and unimpressive. It wasn't invisible, but it was ignored. We were kindred spirits in that way, as laughable as that might sound. Like old friends. Desperate to reconnect. And I was going to be with the fountain one way or another…"

Radio silence. But the silence feels more like anticipation, much like the building tension before a fireworks display on a chilly evening, or rather more like the silence following a large crack when you're stood on a frozen lake. Awaiting the plunge, I decide to continue,

"I wanted to jump into the fountain myself." The stranger's eyes flash when I say this. They widen as he leans forward ever so slightly, those black pearls glinting greedily at what I'm saying, hoping to sample more delicious information, "I'd be lying if I said it hadn't crossed my mind to jump from the top of the shopping centre into that fountain. The very last thing I saw was that disgusting water and my own reflection. I don't know if it was the ripples from the fountain or just the shock at seeing myself, but I really didn't recognise the face I was seeing." I choose not to mention that I was also standing behind the man at the top of the shopping centre. I choose not to mention that my last memory before the splash, was actually of my own hand reaching out towards him – the same man who was shortly in the water. Of course, I am sure that I was only trying to pull the man back from the railing, but I doubt the stranger will see it that way.

"So, after he fell into the fountain, what did you do next?" He says it in such a cold and matter of fact sort of way, I almost feel like chiding him for being so emotionless. Has he no soul at all? Not only does my spinelessness prevent me from calling him out, but I fear that I have used up my opportunities to stall.

"Well – I – I did nothing. What could I do?"

"So, according to your story, a man falls right at your feet, and you do nothing?"

"He was already done for! There was nothing I could've done! You can't raise the dead!"

"He wasn't dead though, was he?"

"What do you mean? Of course he was…"

"He spoke to you, didn't he? What did he say to you? Tell me what he said to you."

"Why are you asking if you think you know the answers?"

"Tell me."

"He didn't say anything, he was dead!"

"Tell me." Tears are pouring down my face now and they aren't cathartic, they're agonising. I've long since lost the opportunity to pretend I can hold my own against this foe. My heart feels like it's going to burst out of my chest, that's if the ringing in my ears doesn't split my head apart first.

I'm lost and nobody is here to help me. I wish somebody would help me,

"He asked me to help him."

"And what did you do?" It's too late to lie now.

"I just stared at him."

"Why? Why did you do it?"

"Why? Because I was scared, I didn't know what to do!"

"No. That's not what I mean. You know that's not what I mean."

The ringing is so high now, I can hardly hear him at all, I'm just reading his lips at this point, even the storm is muffled by this grating dog whistling. But I can feel the house shaking. I'm so dizzy but I can see the cracks in the walls. I can now see the black mould devouring them like a parasitic worm, starving a dying animal of its last ounce of strength. I must be mistaken, but I swear I can see it growing and moving by the second. These walls I had created to house my lies and protect me from what I have really been hiding from are crumbling around me; and creeping, no, whispering beneath this cacophony of menacing and ugly sound, I hear the question I'd been fearing the most.

"Why did you push him?"

6

I don't remember how I got here. I don't remember moving into this house. I can't remember my father's face. I don't know who this stranger is – I don't know who I am. The only thing I can remember is that God forsaken day at the fountain.

That was the day that the rain started.

I can only pray that the stranger will grant me the liberty of pausing to introspect before I answer his damning question. It can be quite liberating to face your deepest fears, if not a little intimidating. Sometimes these things we push to one side can weigh you down so much so that you find yourself unable to move at all, paralysed in the same spot for years on end like an old, forgotten statue heavily fortified by years of bird droppings - cocooned in a crust of someone else's filth. Frozen in time and in shit. Each tick of the clock is louder than the one before it, but as the noise persists, you get better at ignoring such distractions. Each sunset comes sooner than the last, but you turn your back and face the wall, choosing instead to focus on the shadows cast by your own useless body. And then one day, without realising it, the sunrises cease altogether, and you are submerged in darkness, without knowledge of when the last sunset was. At that point, you can't even see your shadow anymore. You're alone. No longer distracted, you're forced to ask, what happens next? What happens when the sun threatens to never rise again? I am reminded of the saying that it's darkest before the dawn, but I haven't seen dawn for months. I convince myself that I despise the rain and dread the idea of being trapped in this house, but the true terror lies in what will happen when it stops? What will I be forced to do then? I feel like I'm living in a pocket dimension where the only future I can see shows me a land where there is no sun. And as grim as that view has been, this purgatory has become a haven. Time has stopped, and if I stay here, I can live forever. With that notion however, there is also a daunting implication, a promise even, that I'll never see tomorrow. So why wouldn't I just stay in here for as long as I can?

Avoiding these issues doesn't always start as a cowardly endeavour. Often times when acknowledging you've done something shameful, putting it on the back burner can be a useful tool to allow yourself time to grow and to change so that when you do eventually come to face these demons, you're far better equipped to vanquish them. But if I keep putting it off until 'tomorrow', can I ever honestly claim that I am a slayer of these demons. I am simply creating more layers of lies which I claim are there to protect me. But in truth they simply exist to suffocate me.

My intention from the start was to hide from what I had done until I was ready to take responsibility and face retribution for my sins.

I, however, have grown too comfortable in this state of stagnation. Instead of arming myself with the courage I need and putting to practice what I quietly preach, I choose to wear the uniform of an honest and pure hearted person. But I realise now that there isn't a time where I have ever demonstrated these values, it's stolen valour of the highest degree. These walls, which I told myself were always meant to be temporary, have decayed and weakened, and countless nights and days of rain (I can no longer differentiate between the two) have only softened the foundations which weren't built to carry the house for so long. Along the way, I have forgotten that this is not my home – it is a house - it is a prison that I designed to detain me until I face the music. And although it is only a prison by my own definition, that doesn't make me a bad person. It doesn't make me a criminal. I am simply another victim of my own weak mind! So now that I hear the trumpets; I must be the man I am supposed to be.

I am done. I am done being a victim. Done being passive. For the first time in my life, I am ready to take action. I'm ready to throw the first punch.

"He had it coming."

"Is that your admission of guilt?" The self-righteous prick has appointed himself as the judge here. I doubt it'll be long before he assumes the role of executioner as well. That's all he's wanted this whole time.

"I am not the villain here. If you knew what it was like to be me, you'd understand. Fuck it. I don't need you to understand – I – I don't need your approval." I see the rage in his eyes as I say this, he can smell blood, but I don't really care - I hope he chokes on it. I can almost feel my cowardice being replaced by strength, or maybe it's anger.

"Do you approve of what you did?"

"Well – that's not important! I have done plenty of things I am not proud of. But this was something I had to do. He looked just like me, for God's sake! He had my face. How did he also have her? Why couldn't I have her? Anyone! You couldn't possibly imagine how lonely it is being me. Every minute you toil along with all these thoughts just hoping, no, praying that somebody will warm you with their attention or even just a smile, just a fleck of acknowledgement that I am a human being. That is all I have ever wanted. But no. I'm invisible. Until I saw her. I knew at that very moment that she was mine; she was meant for me. And the fact that she was with him instead of me - well - that was all the permission I needed to act. I was performing a duty. It's his own fault anyway. If he was down on the ground floor with her, this never would have happened. I saw him holding her hand and knew that he had to go. When he left her on her own, I followed. I was a go getter back then. I must have been – I saw my opportunity and I took it. I honestly believe that that was the biggest loss that day. Fuck that guy, the biggest loss for me that day, was the loss of my ability to see what I want and to take it instead of allowing life to watch me wither away into non existence. I followed him to the top and after he went over the railing, I went down to see the damage. It's as simple as that." He barely changes his facial expression as I unload this on him, and as I watch him, waiting for him to come to my way of thinking, I clench my jaw. It appears he hasn't been moved to a state of understanding whatsoever. He looks more irritated than anything else.

"You might attempt to justify your actions, but I have no sympathy for you. You know that what you've done is wrong. It's downright disgusting in fact. You might've locked yourself away in here, wearing this meek demeanour while speaking in your cowardly voice, and you might don the mask of a simple, feeble loser, but that one display of sheer unbridled evil betrays any kind of 'poor me' persona you are trying to give off. You're sick, and sadly that doesn't mean that you're able to be cured. Your type of evil is a terminal and infectious kind of disease and, worst of all, you still try to defend what you've done even after admitting it out loud." He talks about masks but his is slipping, the bastard. His sterile and emotionless act is failing him as I can see the emotion on his face. I can see him beginning to feel the pain that I have felt. It feels like victory. It feels good. I take his condemnation as praise and his anger is rocket fuel.

"Did you know this man personally? Why does it matter what I did, more importantly, what the hell does it have to do with you anyway?" He looks close to tears when I say this. And I feel nothing as I stare back at him. Into him. "If he was anything like me, he would have wanted it to happen anyway." His black eyes are powerless as I lock onto them. He actually looks down at his feet before he replies.

"I have relived what you did to that man every single day since it happened. But in spite of that, I still harboured hope, albeit a tiny sliver, that you would show signs that you'd changed and maybe that there was a possibility you could be saved. But who am I kidding? There was never a chance. You're a coward, and since that day all I have thought about in the fleeting moments of peace I experience - all I have been able to focus on in those short instances where your vile actions are absent from my mind is one thing, and one thing only. My sole purpose has remained the same. My only goal is to kill you."

The rain has stopped. I look to the TV, hoping the newsman has some words of inspiration for me, maybe he has something to back me up. But the TV is turned off.

It's not even plugged in.

There is no plug. And even though it should be a shocking revelation to learn that somebody intends to kill you, it somehow isn't that much of a surprise to hear it aloud. Seeing the black TV screen, thick with dust, unused for God knows how long, I can't help but laugh. I don't know how I didn't notice this before. The stranger just raises an eyebrow at me. And the little chuckle I have been trying to contain grows until it's a cackle, and then it grows more until it's a hoarse and throaty laugh. It keeps growing until it's an unrestrained, maniacal roar, and I do this while staring at the stranger. I don't break eye contact, and I don't blink – it's not so much that I'm laughing at him as much as I am laughing at myself, the nausea and headache that staring at him gives me only fuels this hysteria. The dull throb in my stomach has become enjoyable to me, and now I can't help but laugh about this situation I find myself in.

I hear the rain and it serves as an off switch to my laughter

– but it's different this time – the rain is in the house. No. Wait, it's not rain…fuck! It's the tap! I break eye contact from the fool in front of me, to look over to the bathroom door – water is trickling out from underneath and another heavy bout of raucous laughter crashes over the last like the coming of the tide.

Turning back to him, I shrug my shoulders and snort away the snot that is pooling on my top lip. I wipe the tears too, but the stranger doesn't see the funny side.

"Now I'm going to need you to come outside with me." He stands directly in front of me, but I'm not intimidated. The idiot has already revealed his hand, that's a rookie error. I know what he intends to do. Being so open was a mistake on his part. Then, with a level of strength I expected him to have, but didn't really think he'd actually use, he clamps hold of my arm with his thick, gnarled fingers and he digs in.

"It's time." He's absolutely right, it is time. I've been waiting for this moment since the stranger announced himself to me. I draw back my free hand and whip it firmly and tightly over his ear. This bull of a man staggers backwards, and now I sense that the momentum has shifted. I watch a small ribbon of blood trickle down his cheek. That's the ticket. As he stumbles back, loosening his grip on my arm, I take him by the collar and drag him over the coffee table, hearing his legs scrape across the sharp edge of the table followed by an agonised snarl jutting through his gritted teeth. I can't squander the opportunity to capitalise on having the upper hand, so I carefully and quickly work around the table in order to get a better angle to deliver some serious damage. I raise my foot high enough so that I can reach maximum velocity when I slam my heel straight back down onto his face. I hear his teeth shatter and there's a muffled pop as his jaw breaks. His mouth hangs open and he attempts to speak, but no words come out. All that comes out is a stringy red paste and bubbling, gurgling moans. As he spits out more shards of his broken teeth, he grabs hold of my shin and with his vice like grip, it feels like he will successfully snap it in half. I've got to give it to him, he is one tough bastard. I drop my knee onto his chest, knocking the wind out of his lungs and spraying his blood all over my face. The metallic goo is bitter as I stick my tongue out to my lip briefly to taste it. I'm disgusted of course, but I want to sample every moment of this.

I want to remember it all. I then drive my elbow, backed by my bodyweight, into the centre of his ugly face. Not satisfied with the concave dent on the bridge of his nose, I rise to my feet and lug his massive head over to the corner of the table and with great effort, slam his face repeatedly onto the razor edge. I am unable to look at the fruits of my labour as I perform this task, but the squelching sound and eventual lack of moaning tells me that I have been successful in nullifying the threat this man poses. I allow his head to drop to the floor, but I can't bring myself to look at the damage. Annoyingly, I catch a glimpse of the pulpy mess that is now his face.

I really don't want to see that mess, I'm not a savage after all.

I turn to face the window and notice that I am no longer finding this situation funny. I don't really know what I feel. This numbness is deeply unsettling. I look around the room, I look at the mould on the wall, the cracks – I look at the water, now tinged with brown and red, growing in volume on the floor – I look at my sofa and the imprint on the cushions. He slotted in like a Tetris piece, a perfect fit. I look with sadness knowing I won't sit on it again, and then I look back out the window. I am unable to turn my attention to the pile of mincemeat on the floor, however. Maybe I do feel an inkling of guilt, but it would be remiss of me not to utilise my extreme efficiency at waving off these intense feelings, so I'll go along with it. Besides, there are bigger issues at hand - It's still raining, and I know that my house is no longer fit to protect me from it. So, I think it's time to go outside.

It's going to get me eventually. It's already entered my home and I can only keep it at bay for so long, so I think now is as good a time as any to go outside and get some fresh air.

I walk with the gait of someone who has been bed bound for months. At first, the little steps towards the door are uncomfortable and unnatural, but each step is easier than the one before it. Unlike the last time I came to my front door, I look around with more freedom. I see things that I didn't see earlier. There are two picture frames hung wonkily on the dirty wall. One is a grainy image of a grown man and a little boy, although I'll be damned if I recognise either of them. The older man is stern faced and strong looking, I can't help but notice how serious he looks. There's no joy or patience in his eyes, which informs me as to why the little boy is such a weak, sickly-looking thing, with tears strewn down his cheeks. His knobbly knees are the thickest parts of his spindly legs which poke out of his tattered shorts like broken toothpicks. His poorly fitting sweatshirt does nothing to hide his rounded shoulders which give him a hunched and frail look. The boy looks close to death. I can't imagine who would take a picture like this, because it certainly doesn't appear to be capturing an enjoyable moment. More intriguing to me is why is it here in my hallway? The other picture frame is empty. Or at least it seems to be at first, upon closer inspection it appears to be the empty frame of a smashed mirror. The small shards of silvery, reflective glass hit the garish light from my lamp creating little rainbow strobe lights. I run my finger back and forth along the shards, partially hoping that it'll draw blood. I am unsuccessful in doing so.

Along the corridor the dust build up is painfully noticeable – I still have no clue how long I've been in here. Cobwebs and mould have made this their domain, and as I look around in disgust, I see a pair of filthy boots coated in a fungal frost and tossed haphazardly beside the front door. I chuckle to myself thinking how they would've been useful when I disposed of the stranger just before, but they'll certainly be of more use outside. Sliding my feet into these damp boots I notice the pool of stinking water slowly chasing me down the hallway. Its colour doesn't allow me to distinguish whether it's from the oozing plasma of the stranger's head, or whether it is a fault of the plumbing. Irrespective of its unpleasant origin, it seems my time is limited, and I will have to compose myself more quickly than I'd hoped.

I have a momentary bout of panic as I reach out towards the door handle. Perhaps foolishly, I have a fear that he will be stood on the other side again, but obviously I know that's nonsense. He is of no threat to me – I'm on my own now. And besides, I've made huge strides. I mustn't relapse into those volatile shifts in mood. I'm better than that now. Despite this, it's strange to me how hollow this whole situation feels. I should be experiencing a sense of accomplishment having overcome this foe, but I feel nothing. Aside from the fear of the unknown, I feel no kind of jubilation or pride over what I've done. I suppose it's typical that I have doubts over whether this victory is a pyrrhic one or not, but that's not where my focus should lie right now; my focus is on whatever exists on the other side of that door.

I sincerely hope there is nothing out there.

The door clicks.

Then it swings open.

I don't know why I am surprised but seeing the rain without the protective layer of glass between us is unnerving. I guess there's nothing stopping me now. I don't even have to think about my next step – my body takes care of it so that

I don't have to. I don't look back at the house, I simply head down the black road, flanked by identical square block houses, more like cells than homes, as these rotten boots carry me along the drenched road.

There is no moonlight to guide me, not that my body needs guidance anyway, I already know where I'm headed…I'd rather not think about it though.

The streetlamps are lined in pairs alongside the road, and until now they had been turned off completely. But each time I reach the next pairing of lights, they click on, but the light only ever shines as far as the next set. I don't know if they sense me coming, but by turning on only moments before I reach them, I can never see what it is I'm walking towards, or what's further down the road. The end is shrouded in darkness. I try to avoid thinking about what lies at the end of this road – any distraction would be welcomed if it prevents me from turning back and heading to the house.

The bulbs are so bright. They're a glaring surgical white light, very similar to the lamp in my house. The stuffiness I felt earlier when I let the stranger into my house remains. It is oddly claustrophobic out here, like the air is almost too thick to breathe, and with my broken and bent nose, I have to breathe a noisy, wheezing breath through my mouth in order to get by. In no time at all, I am drenched in rain and sweat, and I wipe my forehead with the back of my hand to prevent it from blinding me – not that I need to see where I'm going anyway. The sweat stings the small cuts on my hand – another welcome distraction.

As I walk this seemingly endless road, I am intrigued by the equally long row of identical houses. This string of houses makes me doubt what I'm really seeing. It's almost as though I am not moving at all. I'm walking and moving, but nothing around me seems to change. I look through these windows, expecting (but not hoping) to see some kind of movement or life, but I don't see a single light coming from the houses. Not a flicker, not a breath, not a sound. What a relief. The last thing I need are more judging eyes probing and analysing me. It's only me and I am rather proud of myself with how calm I am remaining during this venture outside. The old me would've turned around and headed straight back into the open jaws of my house. Then again, I don't want to return to there, I don't even want to look back. I can't pretend that it wasn't fear which drove me out of that wretched hovel in the first place. This obviously isn't the first time my own actions have terrified me, and despite me trying to do the right thing by coming outside, it has been initiated by me running away from yet another cruel act.

The next coupling of streetlamps click on.

And there it is again - more ringing. It's at a low level, but it's definitely there.

I promised to myself that there would be no more lies. I didn't run out of there because I was scared of what I had done. I've done worse before.

The streetlamps click. Like they're counting my steps, or maybe they're counting down.

The stranger had that coming to him anyway, I can't really pretend that I feel guilty about what I did.

Click.

Besides, I felt the strength of that brute when he grabbed me, hell, I felt the strength of him when he first stood in front of me. I can feel the stomach pains right now.

Click.

That didn't hurt him. Who am I kidding? It probably only pissed him off.

Click.

Reality is much grimmer than my imagination.

Click.

And I know the real reason I'm scared.

Click.

I'm scared because I know he isn't out for the count.

Click.

That's where I'm headed isn't it?

Click.

I'm here. I've reached my destination so to speak.

I can see now why I didn't need to think about where I was walking, this was always where I was supposed to end up. I didn't want to have it festering in my mind either, because I already knew where my feet would take me, and if I'd thought about it too hard, he would know too. But what does it matter?

He already does know.

That'll be why he's standing here in front of me.

Together again. The stranger, me, and the fountain.

7

He's smiling that shit eating grin of his again. It makes my skin crawl, and I now realise why it is that I feel this way. It isn't that he's miraculously appeared outside by the fountain, miles from the house. That can't be why I'm feeling this way. It isn't the fountain, which is somehow here, miles away from the shopping centre I remember it being housed in. It isn't even that the stranger doesn't have any additional facial injuries whatsoever, despite what I remember doing to him in the house. No, what shocks me the most is that he doesn't look like a stranger at all now that he's smiling at me. It's a smug smile, one I've seen multiple times tonight, but it's only now that I recognise it. And that's it. I think that I know the stranger.

"You know, it's sad that you constantly choose to focus on how isolated you are. You speak of loneliness, but you were never alone, not really. We despise each other, and I know the feeling is mutual, but I would be lying if I said I wasn't a bit disappointed at your dismissal of my presence. You go on and on and on about how easy it is to create your own fantasies but when you commit to one for long enough, you forget where reality starts and where the story ends. You indulged in such fantasy for so long, I can only assume you were pretending when you wished to put that way of living behind you. All the fabrications and the myths you told yourself were just for comfort. You want to face the truth, you say. But then when you're face to face with reality you run scared." He walks towards me, and I notice the little puddles don't move as his filth encrusted boots thud into them. "Now, I've tried multiple different approaches. I tried doing nothing. I thought you'd come to make your own decision; I thought you'd make the right choice, but you chose stagnation while I looked on from the shadows. So, then I had to intervene. I tried a cocky and confident approach, one that I knew you would've both feared and admired. Fear is of course the emotion which courses through your very being like the blood in your veins. It's your sole motivator, we both know that. And then I tried being the 'nice guy', the kindly, protective father figure which, again, I knew you craved. Because you're nothing but a follower. A simple drone who doesn't move without instruction because he's scared of the steps he may take without someone else's guidance. God forbid you ever point the finger at yourself when you misstep! And as bad as that is, the glimmer of hope was your awareness of that particular flaw. It's almost admirable that you at least recognise where you're a failure. I genuinely believed that I could nurture that little seed so that maybe you could grow and change. There was hope after all! But nothing could prepare me however for the lows you could fall to. The desperation you've shown so that you can avoid justice has been truly remarkable. Simply acknowledging your flaws isn't enough. It doesn't rectify any wrongdoing by pointing out where you falter if you continue acting in that way to serve your own cowardly purposes. There's no nobility in being aware of your shortcomings, if those very shortcomings are justification for your inaction. I thought that by holding a mirror up to your face, I might be able to get you to cooperate, but lo and behold, that attitude only brought out a level of defiance I never thought you were capable of," he might actually talk me to death if he carries on at this rate. "So defiant that you deny the reality looking right at you. You still don't know who you're talking to. And I know you're not really listening to what I'm saying here. So, I'll address you in language you understand – you are the weakest person I know. The most repugnant and cowardly lowlife I have ever had the displeasure of meeting, and yet you actually countered my efforts to help you with, dare I say it, a backbone? You hit back at me, and obviously you failed in the process. But it isn't your failure that gets me, that's the one thing you excel at, perhaps the funniest part of all is that you honestly thought you could get rid of me." These words don't hurt me. I've been saying this to myself the whole time. I've been attacking myself ever since I pushed that guy into the fountain. This is nothing new, it's just a different voice. But he's not trying to hurt me. He's trying to convince me of something, "You know that you can't hurt me. You aren't that stupid to think you could just physically dispose of me. No – you knew this would end up here, it was always just a matter of time. And that brings me back to this." He waves his hands with a flourish, gesturing toward the fountain behind me. "What do you think you're doing here? Why do you think we're both stood alongside this monstrosity?" I turn and watch the water in the fountain trickling over the brim as the rain pummels into it. It almost seems like the rain is more intense over the area surrounding the fountain. I can't summon the strength to look into the pool though, I am still terrified by what I am almost certain will be looking back at me from beneath the surface of the water.

"I know he's in there." It's not cold, but the weather is causing me to shiver and feel sick, I'm sure of it.

"He?"

"The man! The one I pushed into the fountain, the man I killed! I can't face him, I can't. Please don't make me." I look at the stranger once more, staring, no, pleading into his eyes, but my head is splitting apart, the noise from the ringing is unbearable, the shame is palpable. And yet he is so calm. He looks down at the ground while pinching the bridge of his nose and curtly shaking his head.

"Maybe I gave you a little too much credit. Or maybe I misspoke. In that case, let me be crystal clear to you, ok? I feel it all. All of your pain. It's my pain too. That's why I wanted you to come out in the rain with me." He steps toward me, and his clothes are bone dry. He wraps his arm around my shoulders and grips lightly, gently turning me towards the fountain me. "Look in there. You won't see that poor soul you killed that day." He gestures with an open palm down towards the water in the fountain; the rainfall causes the water to jump and spit, giving it the quality of being alive. I'm still too nervous to look in. "Please. Look into the fountain."

My blood freezes as I look down and tense up instantly. Seeing my reflection for what feels like the first time in years, I can no longer hear the rain, nor can I feel the stranger's hand on my shoulder. The ringing has gone as well.

I observe the hideous face looking back at me with mild disgust, the crooked nose, the swollen and protruding browbone, and thick lumps of scar tissue etched all over like tattoos. It's more monster than man. I wait for it to change into something else, hoping that this is just a mistake on my part, but it just stares back at me with a terrified look. It looks at me like I'm the monster. I touch my face and the reflection does the same.

I spring back from the fountain and I'm stumbling, but I'm not disorientated, my head also isn't spinning and the absence of stomach pain or a high pitched ringing is proving to be more of a distraction than their presence would usually be. I suppose I am seeing clearly. Good God, I wish I was blind! I back away looking at the fountain, not wanting to turn my back in case the reflection grabs me and pulls me in – but then I back into the stranger. He's still here. Turning to face him with a different perspective, I can now look him in the eye, pain free and without fear. Having now seen my own face, I look at his and in a desperate bid to see if my eyes are lying to me, I ask the only question I can think of to confirm my madness.

"Who are you?"

Behind him, like ants in a colony, gaunt faceless figures pour out from their respective houses alongside the road, wild and rough looking, jostling to and fro, knocking their fragile and bony limbs against one another, apparently unable to see their soulless brethren without eyes. Despite this, they never walk out towards the road. They just mill around bumping into each other, their sallow flesh pulled taut on their bones, bruising upon each collision.

Apparently as interested in the answer as I am, they gather afront their houses, turning those smooth, blank canvases that are their 'faces' towards me. I cannot see them clearly from this distance, but their rabbling movement and general roughhousing subsides, and I feel a rising anticipation that they will speak. I have no idea what these alien looking creatures would say if they could talk, and their absence of a mouth makes this thought not only unlikely, but implausible.

I am not prepared therefore, when they erupt into a chorus of offensive low groaning. The noise is thunderous, sounding as though it emerged from the deepest depths of the ocean rather than from the throats of some meek creature. this grating cry is physically painful to the ear, and I wonder how they're able to produce sound like that. The rain is pouring down like hellfire at this point and the combination of these two sounds together creates an unholy duet which makes my skin itch and stomach crawl.

I won't be able to even hear what the stranger says at this rate, and this is ultimately the one question where I want – need – to know the answer.

Perhaps he didn't hear me over the sound of them.

I scream at the top of my lungs, "WHO ARE YOU?" He simply smiles at me.

Then he grabs my throat. Pushing me effortlessly over to the fountain by the neck, immune to my flailing blows at his arms and ribs. It's not like before – everything I'm throwing at him either misses or crumples on impact. It's not how I imagined it would be, but I suppose reality is grimmer than my imagination. All I can do as he pushes me backwards towards the fountain is stare at him, his facial expression doesn't change, and in the panic, I wonder if I am looking at a mad man or if I'm looking in a mirror.

He's still smiling at me. Even as my legs buckle against the side of the fountain, he just looks at me with sympathy on his face, like he's doing me a favour of some sort.

The water is freezing. I suck in and bite at it as I push back in desperation. As I force my head above water while choking, I am just able to take a big breath of air before he piledrives my body back underneath. There's nothing vicious about what he's doing, however. There's no blood, no anger. It's procedural. Efficient.

And I am only making it more difficult by resisting this much. So why bother? I don't wish to turn this into a spectacle for those nameless, faceless abominations looking from afar, so I don't see why I shouldn't just accept what is happening. That's what this whole evening has been about anyway.

Everything that I've done has led me to this point, and I suppose I'm in a privileged position where I can wonder if I would've done things differently had I known that this was my destination. This is the same dilemma for anyone really. I'm not special.

Seeing as this was always going to be where I would end up, I don't think it would matter if I had done things otherwise. All that would change is that I might have had more things to look back on, it would've been cheap entertainment. But how much is that worth? I don't feel like I've learned anything from my life.

THE RAIN

It's all been a desperate sprint to the finish, and if tonight has taught me anything, it's that it's all been for nothing. For that, I can be thankful that it may soon be over.

I look up through the hazy lens of the water, and I don't see any friends, family or loved ones. I can't even see those ghouls looking at me like I'm some kind of exhibition at the zoo.

All I can see is that blank face of the stranger. It's a face I hate. It's hideous. And, as I stare into what are supposed to be the 'windows to the soul', fully at peace now I have accepted what's coming, I know that that phrase rings true. Looking into the black nothingness of his eyes, I can forgive him for this because he has no soul. I should know after all — they are my eyes.

It's a peaceful feeling under here, I've let go and have taken in the water.

It burns at first. The first unanswered breath forces me to beg for another, but being fully surrounded prevents my lungs from taking in the oxygen it so dearly craves. The water sears my windpipe causing me to convulse in complete and utter agony. Then it coats my lungs like lava, and I want to break free and escape this hell, but the stranger's grip keeps me from fighting against this for too long.

The panic washes away eventually — it always does in the end. It must be said that it's comforting to have absolute silence, I can't hear that crowd from across the road, I don't feel any sickness, I don't have to think about tomorrow, and under here I feel completely weightless.

I also can't feel any hands on my throat anymore, or maybe he's let go. I don't know. But I still see him floating above me — rather, I see myself just above the surface. It's a strange funhouse mirror really, because he seems to be crying, and I know that's not something I would do, so I smile. He just smiles back at me. It's as uncomfortable as the tears.

But who am I to complain? I'm at peace. It's so tranquil down here, that I might be able to do the thing that I haven't done in what feels like a lifetime now – I might get some sleep.

I still feel weightless, and I no longer have the urge to breathe as my body apparently has no use for that feature anymore. I am simply gazing at this sky in pure bliss. There isn't a star in sight, nor is there any moonlight. There are only the gentle charcoal smudges and dark clouds convulsing as the wind blows them onward.

In an instant, the stranger is gone, and it seems like the little undulations in the water caused by the rain have also stopped. In fact, there is nothing around me at all, it's all been washed away. That's fine however, I still have the sky.

Even the fountain is gone now too, and I lie here, floating weightlessly, looking at the clouds above.

They contort into wondrous shapes and amongst the folds of darkness I see flecks of grey, like the mottled fur of some ageing beast. I wonder if there is anyone else who is seeing this - it's truly beautiful.

And it's always reliable. My one constant. It's always been there and it's always growing. It's actually getting closer as I watch it, and I genuinely think that someday it'll grow so big that it consumes me and anyone else living here.

That doesn't scare me though. It's a foregone conclusion.

It's always the same, it goes from black to grey, then to black again.

THE RAIN

Printed in Great Britain
by Amazon

32893691R00046